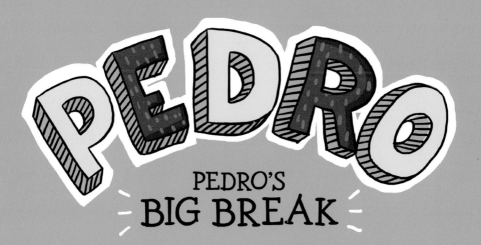

PEDRO

PEDRO'S
BIG BREAK

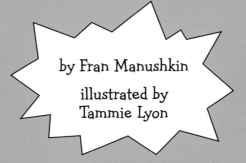

by Fran Manushkin

illustrated by
Tammie Lyon

PICTURE WINDOW BOOKS
a capstone imprint

Pedro is published by Picture Window Books,
A Capstone Imprint
1710 Roe Crest Drive
North Mankato, Minnesota 56003
www.capstonepub.com

Names: Manushkin, Fran, author. | Lyon, Tammie, illustrator.
Title: Pedro's big break / by Fran Manushkin; illustrated by Tammie Lyon.
Description: North Mankato, Minnesota: Picture Window Books, [2018] |
   Series: Pedro | Summary: When Pedro breaks his arm racing his bike he has
   to cope with the frustration of wearing a cast for a whole month—but with
   the help of his friends he discovers that there are still fun things to do.

Identifiers: LCCN 2018002734 (print) | LCCN 2018004452 (ebook) |
ISBN 9781515828389 (eBook PDF) | ISBN 9781515828228 (hardcover) |
ISBN 9781515828273 (pbk.)

Subjects: LCSH: Hispanic American boys—Juvenile fiction. | Arm—
Fractures—Juvenile fiction. | Wounds and injuries—Juvenile fiction. |
Friendship—Juvenile fiction. | CYAC: Fractures—Fiction. | Wounds and
injuries—Fiction. | Friendship—Fiction. | Hispanic Americans—Fiction.

Classification: LCC PZ7.M3195 (ebook) | LCC PZ7.M3195 Pch 2018 (print) |
DDC

   813.54 [E] —dc23

LC record available at https://lccn.loc.gov/2018002734

Designer: Kayla Rossow
Design Elements by Shutterstock

Printed and bound in the USA
PA021

Table of Contents

Chapter 1
Pedro Goes Flying

Pedro loved going fast.

Winning bike races was fun.

He told Katie, "Today I can

win my third race in a row.

I just need a big break."

Zoom! The race began.

Pedro rode fast—very fast!

Oops! His bike hit a rock,

and Pedro went flying. He fell

hard on his arm!

The doctor told him, "Your arm is broken, but this cast will help it heal. You'll be fine in four weeks."

Pedro groaned. "This *isn't* the big break I wanted."

Pedro told Katie, "Now I can't go camping. I'll miss sleeping in a tent and eating s'mores and seeing shooting stars."

"I'll draw stars on your

cast," said Katie. "Then you

can see them all the time."

But Pedro still felt sad. He

wasn't fast anymore. He had

to do everything slowly.

Chapter 2

Poor Pedro

Taking a bath was tricky.

Getting dressed was tricky too.

In school, Pedro had to

write with his wrong hand.

Miss Winkle tried to cheer him up. She said, "Your bone will heal in just a few weeks."

Pedro groaned. "I want it to happen faster."

JoJo told Pedro, "Your arm

is broken, but your brain still

works. I bet you will think of

ways to be happy."

But Pedro kept thinking

about the camping trip he was

missing.

No shooting stars!

No scary stories!

No s'mores!

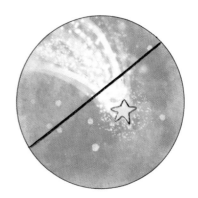

A week later, Pedro's brother Paco woke up in the middle of the night. He told Pedro, "I had a scary dream!" Paco cried and cried.

Pedro wanted to cheer Paco

up. Wrestling always made

him happy, but Pedro couldn't

wrestle.

"What can I do with one

hand?" he wondered.

"Aha!" Pedro smiled.

"I know!"

Pedro made funny shadow
puppets. One hand could do
a lot!

Paco laughed and laughed
and forgot his dream. Soon
he hugged his pillow and fell
asleep smiling.

Chapter 3
Camp-In!

Before he fell back to sleep,

Pedro had another fun idea.

"We can camp in the yard!"

But when Pedro woke up,

it was raining. The ground

was all wet.

"I know," said Pedro. "Let's camp inside. My sheet can be our tent."

"Cool idea," said his dad.

His mom made a campfire out of colored paper.

"A camp needs

ants," said Katie.

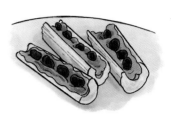

She made ants on a log by

filling celery with peanut

butter and raisins.

"Yum," said Pedro. "Ants

are tasty."

JoJo told scary stories, and
they spooked each other with
flashlights.

Then they ate lots of s'mores.

Pedro said, "All we are

missing are shooting stars."

"No way," said his dad. "I'll

get the telescope. We can see

shooting stars right here."

Pedro's dad placed his
telescope near the window.

"I see them!" Pedro yelled.
"I see shooting stars. Boy, are
they fast!"

Boy, was Pedro happy!

"Next week," said his dad,

"your cast is coming off."

"Yay!" everyone cheered.

Pedro cheered the loudest.

A few weeks later, Pedro was racing again—fast, fast, fast!

"From now on," he said, "I don't want to get any more big breaks."

And so far, he hasn't!

About the Author

Fran Manushkin is the author of many popular picture books, including *Happy in Our Skin; Baby, Come Out!; Latkes and Applesauce: A Hanukkah Story; The Tushy Book; Big Girl Panties; Big Boy Underpants;* and *Bamboo for Me, Bamboo for You!* There is a real Katie Woo—she's Fran's great-niece—but she never gets in half the trouble of the Katie Woo in the books. Fran writes on her beloved Mac computer in New York City, without the help of her two naughty cats, Chaim and Goldy.

About the Illustrator

Tammie Lyon began her love for drawing at a young age while sitting at the kitchen table with her dad. She continued her love of art and eventually attended the Columbus College of Art and Design, where she earned a bachelor's degree in fine art. After a brief career as a professional ballet dancer, she decided to devote herself full time to illustration. Today she lives with her husband, Lee, in Cincinnati, Ohio. Her dogs, Gus and Dudley, keep her company as she works in her studio.

Glossary

broken (BROH-kuhn)—having a crack, such as in a bone

cast (KAST)—a hard plaster covering that supports a broken arm or leg

heal (HEEL)—to get better

s'mores (SMORS)—a dessert made out of toasted marshmallow and pieces of chocolate bar sandwiched between two graham crackers

spooked (SPOOKD)—frightened or scared

telescope (TEL-uh-skope)—an instrument that makes distant objects, such as stars, seem larger and closer

wrestling (RESS-ling)—a sport in which two people try to throw or force each other to the ground

Let's Talk

1. At the beginning of the story, Pedro
    says he just needs a big break to win a
    bike race. What does he mean by "a
    big break"?

2. Have you ever gone camping? Compare
    your camping trip with Pedro's indoor
    camping trip. How were they the same?
    How were they different?

3. How did Pedro feel when he got to race
    his bike again? What details from the
    story tell you how he felt?

Let's Write

1. Make a list of the things that were harder for Pedro to do when he had a cast. Then make a list of the things he could still do with a cast.

2. If you could draw a picture on Pedro's cast, what would you draw? Why?

3. Pretend Pedro is your friend and he's just broken his arm. Make him a card to cheer him up.

JOKE AROUND

If you broke your leg in two places, what would you do?
Stay away from those two places.

Knock knock
Who's there?
Eel.
Eel who?
Eel is what your broken arm will do in that cast!

What do you do for a bird with a broken wing?
Give it special tweet-ment.

Why did the book go to the doctor?
It broke its spine.

How did the frog feel when it had a broken leg?
unhoppy

What is the most musical bone?
the trom-bone

What did the left arm say to the right arm?
"How are you always right?"

THE FUN DOESN'T STOP HERE!

Discover more at www.capstonekids.com

- Videos & Contests
- Games & Puzzles
- Friends & Favorites
- Authors & Illustrators

Find cool websites and more books like this one at www.facthound.com. Just type in the Book ID: 9781515828228 and you're ready to go!